The Secret Puppy

The Secret Puppy

by Holly Webb
Illustrated by Sophy Williams

tiger tales

For Zoe

tiger tales

5 River Road, Suite 128, Wilton, CT 06897
Published in the United States 2016
Originally published in Great Britain 2012
by Little Tiger Press
Text copyright © 2012 Holly Webb
Illustrations copyright © 2012 Sophy Williams
ISBN-13: 978-1-58925-483-1
ISBN-10: 1-58925-483-X
Printed in China
STP/1800/0073/0815
10 9 8 7 6 5 4 3 2 1

For more insight and activities, visit us at www.tigertalesbooks.com

Chapter One

Daisy jumped out of the car, looking eagerly around the field. It was the first time she'd been camping, and she was really excited.

"Is this our tent?" she asked her dad, gazing at the big green and red tent they'd parked next to. "It's huge!"

Dad nodded. "The lady on the phone said it can sleep six. So that means you and Oliver can each have a room to sleep in."

"A pod," Oliver corrected him. "They're called pods, Dad."

Daisy rolled her eyes. Just because Oliver had been camping with Cub Scouts, he thought he knew everything. He always thought he was more clever than Daisy, anyway, being a year older than her. Oliver had enjoyed Cub Scout camp so much that he'd begged and begged for them to go camping during the summer. But Daisy didn't mind. Usually they rented a cottage by the seaside, and it was nice to do something different. Riverside Farm had a lot of things to do, and many animals to make friends with. Mom wasn't quite so convinced about tents, though.

She'd finally agreed to camping, but she'd insisted that they went to the kind of campsite where the owners would put up one of their tents for you, if you wanted. Oliver had said that was cheating.

"Pods, sorry, Mr. Camping Expert." Dad lugged one of the big boxes out of the car. They might not have needed to bring their own tent, but there was still a lot of stuff. They'd rented a little gas stove and some cooking equipment from the campsite as well, but they'd had to bring sleeping bags and lawn chairs to sit on. Dad had said he couldn't cope with sitting on the ground for a week. Then there was all the food and clothes. Mom had insisted on bringing raincoats and boots, just in case.

"Can we go and explore?" Daisy asked hopefully. "Look at the river! It runs right by our tent!" She'd known there was a river running through the campsite – the name was a bit of a giveaway – but she hadn't realized they would be camping so close to it. She could imagine curling up to sleep in their tent, hearing the water rushing along. "There's a bridge to get to the rest of the farm. Oh, and look! Ducks! There might even be baby ones. And I have to go and see the horses!"

"I want to go and look at the pool," Oliver put in. "We won't be long, Mom."

Mom shook her head. "Not yet. You can explore soon, I promise. We need to unpack, and then Dad and I will come with you to have a look around. I need to know where you're going to be before I let you take off."

Oliver looked like he was about to

argue, but then he sighed and grabbed an armful of sleeping bags out of the car. "Can I have this room?" he asked, unzipping one of the doors off the main living area. The three bedrooms stuck out at the sides and the back of the tent, and there was a sort of open canopy at the front, which they could cook under if it was raining.

"I thought it was called a pod," Daisy said sweetly, dodging the sleeping bag he flung at her. "If you're having that one, can I have this one in the back?"

Dad nodded. "I don't see why not. They're all the same size."

"And that leaves us the furthest away from Oliver and his snoring," Mom pointed out.

Daisy picked up the sleeping bag

Oliver had thrown at her (it was hers) and unzipped the door to the back bedroom. It was actually quite big, she realized, feeling surprised. She'd expected the tent to be tiny, but her bedroom even had a back door! She unzipped it and peeked out, smiling to herself as she saw the river running along a few feet behind the tent. She wasn't going to tell Oliver she had her own secret door — he'd want to swap.

Luckily, it didn't take too long to unpack — Daisy didn't have to put her clothes away, since there wasn't anywhere to put them. She spread out her sleeping bag, thinking that she was actually looking forward to going to bed. She'd never slept next to a river before.

"Daisy? Are you ready? Should we go and take a look around?" her mom called. Daisy jumped up, stepped out of the pod, and zipped the door closed behind her.

"Will you be all right, sleeping in there by yourself?" her mom asked a little anxiously, but Daisy beamed at her.

"It's perfect! Why wouldn't I be all right? It's only like having my own room at home, Mom."

Her mom nodded. "I suppose we're very close to you, if you do get nervous."

Daisy giggled. "I could probably reach a hand out of my bedroom door and tickle your feet if I stretched."

"So what should we go and see first?" Dad asked. "There's a little shop that sells ice cream. Should we do that?"

"Ice cream?" Oliver poked his head out of his pod. Daisy nodded eagerly. It was very warm in the tent; an ice cream sounded perfect.

Mom looked at the little map she'd picked up when they'd arrived at the campsite. "Once we've done that, and we've had a quick look around, I don't mind if you two go off on your own, as long as you promise to tell us where you're going and be back when we say."

Daisy smiled. She didn't usually get to go to places on her own, although Oliver sometimes walked to school with his friends now that he was in middle school.

Being at the campsite was like a big adventure.

They walked past lots of other tents on the way to the shop, which was part of the old farm buildings. They'd all been converted now, with a little food shop, and a gift shop, and a craft area that did workshops they could sign up for. Daisy really wanted to try the jewelry one.

There were quite a few other boys around — including a couple about Oliver's age playing football outside a tent close to theirs. But Daisy couldn't see many girls, except for a few little ones. Still, she didn't mind. There was a lot of stuff to do, and she was looking forward to exploring on her own.

"No one brought dogs with them,"

she said to Dad, as they walked along the line of tents. Daisy loved dogs, and she'd thought that there might be a few staying in tents with their owners.

"I don't think dogs are allowed, are they?" Dad said. "I'm sure I read that somewhere on the website. They might frighten the animals, I suppose."

Daisy sighed, and Dad put an arm around her shoulders. "Don't worry, Daisy. There are a lot of other animals here. Don't forget those piglets, and the horses."

Daisy nodded. She *was* excited about the piglets, but a dog to play with would have been even nicer. She'd been trying to persuade her parents that they should get a dog for a while, but it didn't seem to be working. Mom was worried that their yard wasn't big enough, although Daisy was sure that people with much smaller yards than theirs had dogs. Besides, there was a huge park close to their house, so it didn't really matter. But Mom said that wasn't the same.

She'd tried to get Oliver to help her persuade them, but he didn't really care. He already had a pet, a tarantula called Otto that he'd gotten for his ninth birthday. Daisy hated spiders. If Oliver wanted to upset her, he'd open his bedroom door and pretend he was letting Otto out of his tank. It made Daisy scream. That was one of the good things about camping — Otto couldn't come, either. Oliver had left him with his friend Max while they were gone.

Daisy shuddered, just thinking about the enormous spider. How could Mom and Dad let Oliver have such a horrible pet? And Otto was huge. Not that much smaller than a very small dog, really....

"Come on, slowpoke!" Oliver turned to look back at Daisy, as she started to trail behind the rest of the family. "Don't you want ice cream?"

Chapter Two

"Someone *has* brought a dog; I'm sure I heard it barking as we walked across the yard!" Daisy pulled at her dad's sleeve. "Well, just little dog noises, really — more like whining than barking."

The teenage girl scooping out the ice cream smiled at her. "Those are the puppies you can hear. They're in the stable on the other side of the yard."

"Puppies?" Daisy asked hopefully.

"Uh-huh. German shepherds. My mom breeds them — we've got so much space with all the old farm buildings that the dogs have their own special room. It's the one with the sign over the door that says Riverside German Shepherds."

"Are we allowed to see them?" Daisy said. She loved German shepherds; they were so noble-looking.

"Maybe — you'll have to ask my mom, Julie. You probably met her at the reception desk."

Daisy nodded. The lady who'd given them the map and told them where their tent was — her name was definitely Julie. And she did look a lot like Amy, the girl in the shop, with dark, curly hair. "I'll ask," she told Amy. "Thanks!"

Daisy wasn't usually all that good at asking for things — she was too shy. But for the chance to meet some puppies, she could be brave enough to talk to someone she didn't know.

Once she'd eaten her ice cream, Daisy persuaded Mom to return to the reception area with her, while Dad and Oliver went to look at the climbing wall.

"Hello! Is everything all right? Do you like your tent?" Julie asked them, smiling.

Mom nodded. "It's wonderful. Much bigger than we'd expected." She gave Daisy an encouraging look.

"Would it be okay...," Daisy began. "I mean — please could I see the puppies? Amy said there were puppies."

Julie laughed. "There are. Six of them. They're 10 weeks old now. Do you like dogs?"

"Yes. I'd love to have my own dog. Do you have a lot of them?"

"Usually only Lucy, the puppies' mom, and Sally, her sister. We don't breed very many puppies — just two litters a year. And then we either sell them as pets, or sometimes they go to be working dogs. Many of our puppies are police dogs now."

Daisy nodded. She knew that German shepherds made good police dogs because they could be trained so well. They were used as sniffer dogs, and search and rescue dogs, too.

"Don't they get too big to be pets?" Daisy's mom asked doubtfully.

Julie shook her head, laughing. "No! Well, they are big, I suppose. We have Lucy and Sally in the house with us, when they aren't having puppies and living in the puppy room, and they do take up a lot of the kitchen in their baskets. But to be honest, it all depends on how well-behaved a dog is. If you train a big dog properly, it takes up less room than a small dog!"

It sounded silly, but Daisy knew what Julie meant. Her friend Melissa had a miniature dachshund, who was beautiful but also completely spoiled. Melissa's entire family ran around after her. She definitely took up a *lot* of room....

"I was actually going over to check on the puppies in a minute anyway," Julie said, glancing at her watch. "You can come with me if you'd like."

"Yes, please!" Daisy said eagerly. "Do they need feeding? Puppies need a lot of meals, don't they?"

Julie looked at her in surprise. "I didn't think you had a dog."

Daisy smiled shyly. "Oh, I don't. But I love reading about them. I got a wonderful book all about dogs for Christmas. I've read it four times, and it says lots of stuff about puppies. Are your puppies almost ready to go to new homes if they're 10 weeks old?"

"Yes, their new owners are coming to visit this week and next." Julie came out from behind the reception desk, and led Daisy and her mom back up the path toward the main yard. "We've been lucky. We've made a name for ourselves breeding good-natured dogs. There was an article in the local paper about training police dogs, which had a beautiful photo of two of our puppies with their police handlers. After that, a lot of people wanted a Riverside puppy. All the puppies in this litter will go to people on the waiting list."

"Oh...," Daisy gave a tiny sigh. She had been daydreaming that Mom would fall in love with one of the German shepherd puppies, and she'd finally be able to persuade her to get a dog. She was pretty sure Dad was already coming around to the idea. He had admitted he liked the early-morning walks to get some fresh air before he started work. He and Mom worked together from home, designing websites, and he spent most of his time stuck in front of the computer. Daisy sighed again. There was no point even thinking about it. A dog would be the best thing to take home from a vacation ever, but if the puppies were all reserved, it was no use.

They'd reached the main yard now, and Julie opened the door to the puppy room. "We converted it especially for the dogs, so that they've got a place to run outside as well. Now that it's so hot, we've been able to leave the door open all the time, so they can get some fresh air. And we take them out into our yard, too."

Just inside the room was a wire pen with a gate in it, and stretched out on a fleece blanket was a beautiful German shepherd. She looked exactly like the photos from Daisy's book, with golden brown legs and ears, and a black face and back. She had huge dark eyes, and she was staring thoughtfully at Daisy. She didn't look fierce — just watchful.

And Daisy could understand why. Tumbling around her were four beautiful puppies, and she was making sure that Daisy and her mom were safe to be around them. The puppies, however, weren't worried at all. They bounced over to the edge of the cage and scratched excitedly at the wire. If they stood on their hind legs, they could almost put their noses over the top. Two more puppies dashed in from the outside area and flung themselves at the wire, too, yapping excitedly.

Daisy's mom laughed. "Oh my goodness. I can see why you have them out here instead of in the house...."

"We do bring them into the house, too, to get them used to being around people and to being careful with the furniture," Julie explained. "But not usually all at once. It's a big old farmhouse, but eight German shepherds are a bit much for any home."

"They're beautiful," Daisy breathed. She'd been expecting the puppies to be cute, and they were, but it still wasn't quite the right word for them. Although they were really soft and fluffy, they didn't have round little puppy faces. They already had long German shepherd muzzles and upstanding ears. They weren't just cute — they were *handsome*.

Then one of the puppies put his head to one side and gazed at Daisy. His ears twitched and wriggled. Daisy laughed and crouched down to get a better look.

"Oh, he's got a floppy ear," she said, wishing she could pet it. The puppy was the darkest of the litter, with pretty brownish-gold fur, and black markings on his face, like a sort of curly T-shape that went over his eyes and down his nose.

Julie crouched down next to her. "Handsome, isn't he? Their ears start to straighten up around now; he's just taking a little longer than the others. Sometimes they're about five months old before their ears stand up correctly."

The puppy seemed to know that they

were talking about him. His brothers and sisters had lost interest in Daisy, and went off to chase each other around the pen and play with the toys that were scattered everywhere. But he stayed by the wire, watching her intently with his dark, intelligent eyes.

"What's his name?" she asked Julie.

"Well, we try not to name them, even though it's difficult sometimes. It's nice if their new owners can choose their own names," Julie explained.

"He looks really clever," Daisy said.

"He *is* sweet," Mom agreed.

Daisy looked up at her eagerly, and Mom shook her head. "Don't get too excited! We couldn't have a big dog like that."

"But — we might be able to get a dog? Another kind of dog?" Daisy whispered.

"We're thinking about it," her mom admitted. "Dad would really like a dog, and I had a dog when I was your age. She was named Cola. You and Oliver are old enough to be able to take care of a dog now. So maybe we can think about it when we get home...."

"Oh, Mom!" Daisy flung her arms around her mom's neck.

The puppy by the wire looked up at them, wondering what was going on. His floppy ear straightened up for a second, and then flopped over again. The girl looked down at him, and he licked her hand through the wire and made her laugh. He liked her.

Daisy crouched down by the wire again. "I might be able to have a puppy like you," she whispered.

"You can pet him, if you're gentle," Julie told her, and Daisy slowly stretched out her fingers, so as not to scare the puppy, and rubbed his golden fur. She sighed contentedly.

Julie was smiling. "If you want, Daisy, you might be able to help me with socializing the puppies — getting them used to different people before they go to their new homes."

"Can I, Mom?" Daisy asked hopefully. She had two weeks at Riverside Farm. It was the perfect opportunity to show Mom and Dad what a fantastic dog-owner she would be. She was scratching the puppy behind his velvety ears now, and he was leaning blissfully against the side of the pen.

Mom nodded. "Just don't get too used to German shepherds, Daisy! I know they're beautiful, but if we do get a dog, it'll definitely be something smaller."

Chapter Three

The flop-eared puppy galloped across the grass, and skidded to a halt before he landed in the rose bushes — he knew they were prickly. Then he turned around and galloped the whole way back again. All the puppies loved playing out in the yard. Now that they were getting bigger, they spent a lot of time running around. Julie had given them an old football, and his two sisters were fighting over it in the middle of the lawn. He thought about going to join in, but then he spotted a blackbird landing on top of the old brick wall.

The puppy stalked over, his tail wagging from side to side. He hoped that the bird would come down, so he could get a better look. The blackbird stared back, its head to one side, but it showed no sign of coming any closer. The puppy crept toward the bird, and then made a mad little dash up onto the wall, jumping and scratching at the bricks and barking hopefully. The blackbird fluttered its wings in fright, squawked, and flew away.

"I think you have to sneak up on them a little more to catch them,"

Daisy said behind him. At the sound of her voice, the puppy forgot about the blackbird, and raced over to her, his tail wagging madly. He

planted his big front paws on her knees and did his best to lick her face all over.

"Hello there!" Daisy smiled. They were almost a week into their vacation, and she had visited the puppies every day so far. Oliver had been off doing canoeing and raft-building on the river, but although Daisy had gone to a couple of the craft sessions, she by far preferred playing with the puppies.

Daisy's dad had come to find her the day before, and he'd apologized to Julie for Daisy hanging around the puppy pen all the time.

"Not at all — it's great to have someone else to play with the puppies," Julie had explained. "Most of them are going to family homes, so they need to get used to being around children. Daisy's helping me out! And the puppies love her. She's very patient."

Daisy glowed when Julie said that. She really wanted Mom and Dad to think of her as someone who was good with dogs — someone who could be helpful if *they* got a dog. But most of all she was pleased that Julie thought that the puppies liked her. Especially her favorite puppy, the one with the floppy ear. When no one was listening, Daisy had secretly named him Baxter. It seemed to suit him. She did play with the other puppies, too, but Baxter always came over to her and, if she sat down in the pen, he would snuggle up with his nose on her lap. He'd even fallen asleep like that a couple of times.

Lucy, the puppies' mother, wasn't in the pen with them today. She still spent a lot of time with the puppies, but as they were completely weaned from her milk and eating puppy food, she liked a bit of time off now and then. Julie said that all she did when she wasn't with the puppies was rest in her basket, next to her sister, Sally, looking exhausted. Occasionally she'd get up to get a big drink of water. Daisy thought she must be grateful to do this without three or four puppies coming to see what she was doing and then joining in and splashing her.

That morning, Daisy and Oliver had gone for a walk with Dad down to the nearest village, as they both had some vacation money to spend. Oliver had bought a football, and Daisy had spent some of her money on a pack of puppy treats. It was bulging in her shorts pocket now. She'd asked Julie if it was okay to give them to the puppies, and she had said it was fine, as long as it was only a few at a time.

Just then, Julie came up to the door of the pen. "I was thinking, Daisy, if you'd like, you could take one of the puppies out for a little walk around the yard for me," she suggested. "I need them to get used to seeing a lot of people, and walking on a leash, too. They'll all be going to obedience classes as soon as they get to their new homes, and it'll be good if the leash isn't a complete surprise."

Daisy nodded. That would be amazing — like having her very own dog! "Which puppy do you want me to take?" she asked, hoping it would be Baxter.

"You can choose, as long as I know who you've taken — that way I can make sure they all get a turn. Don't take them out of the yard, though, and only walk them for a few minutes. They need to start small and build up."

Daisy glanced at Baxter. She was

sure he would love the yard. He was such a curious little dog. *Maybe people would think he belonged to me*, she thought. He could be her secret puppy, just for a little while.

Julie gave her a collar and a leash to put on Baxter, and showed her how to fasten it so that it would stay on without being too tight.

Baxter wriggled and whined with excitement as Daisy tried to put the collar on him. He wasn't really sure what was happening, but it was definitely new and different. And Daisy was there. He loved it when she came to play with him. She would spend a long time rolling a ball back and forth for him to chase, or stroking his ears.

Eventually Daisy managed to get the leash on him, and she led Baxter out of the pen, and then out the door to the yard, with the puppy waltzing joyfully around her feet. "Careful, Baxter!" Daisy laughed. "You're going to trip me up." She glanced around to check that Julie wasn't listening. She didn't want her to know that she'd named the puppy — he wasn't hers to name, after all.

"We're going on our first walk!"

Baxter stared at the people in the yard, eating ice cream from the shop, visiting the piglets in their stall, or petting the two horses. Children were running around, laughing and shouting. He'd never seen so many people at once. He was used to Julie and the occasional visitor, but that was all. He stopped jumping around and twitched his tail in a nervous sort of wag.

Daisy crouched down next to him. "It's okay, Baxter. I know it's a little scary. Let's just go around the edge of the yard a bit…." She coaxed him along, being careful not to pull on the leash, until they reached a bench. She sat down, snuggling Baxter up against her knees. She wished she could pick him up and have him on her lap, but Julie had told her that the puppies weren't allowed on the furniture when they went in the farmhouse, because they were going to be just too big when they were older. So she thought it was probably best if he didn't go on benches, either. But she could still cuddle him. *And* give him a reward, she suddenly remembered!

Daisy pulled the foil pack of treats out of her pocket and tore it open, shaking a few into her hand. "Here, Baxter!" She held them out to him.

Baxter sniffed the delicious treats and glanced around. He'd been staring worriedly at the horse that was leaning its head out of its stall and watching him. It was enormous! But the treats smelled so good that he soon forgot to worry. He crunched them happily, and Daisy giggled as his soft, whiskery nose nuzzled against her hand, followed by a wet, velvety tongue — Baxter was making sure he hadn't missed any crumbs.

Daisy sat there enjoying the sunshine, and the admiring glances from the people passing by. She knew she should take Baxter back and give one of the other puppies a turn, like Julie had said. But not just yet....

"Daisy!"

Daisy jumped. She hadn't noticed her mom standing beside the bench. She smiled. "Hi, Mom! I didn't see you."

"I was coming to check if you wanted to go to the craft session this afternoon — they're making friendship bracelets. I thought you might like to take some home for Melissa and Eva."

"Okay." Daisy nodded. "That sounds fun. Thanks." She looked sideways at her mom, feeling slightly worried. Why was she frowning like that?

"Daisy, this is the same puppy again, isn't it?" Her mom sat down next to her, and gently rubbed Baxter's floppy ear. He panted happily, enjoying the attention.

"The same as what…?" Daisy said, stalling. She was pretty sure she knew what her mom meant, but she didn't know why it mattered.

"The one with the floppy ear — the one you're always playing with."

"Yes…. But Julie asked me to take him out and show him the yard. It's to get him used to being on a leash."

"And did she say you could give him the treats, too?" Mom asked her.

"Yes! You know I wouldn't feed him anything without asking!" Daisy protested.

"Mmm. But I don't think Julie meant that you should give treats just to this puppy. Have you taken any of the others out like this?"

"No, but…," Daisy trailed off.

"Daisy, if you fall in love with this puppy, what's it going to be like when we go home? We've got less than a week here now, sweetheart. I don't want you to be sad when you have to leave him." Mom sighed. "And actually, it's not very fair to him, either."

Daisy looked up in surprise. "What do you mean? Baxter really likes me! He looks forward to seeing me, I know he does!"

"Exactly. Dogs get very attached to people, Daisy. Next Saturday he'll be waiting for you to come and see him, and you'll be on your way home!"

Daisy's eyes filled with tears. She'd known she was really going to miss Baxter, but she'd been trying not to think about it. He was her vacation dog — her secret, special puppy, just for these few days.

But she hadn't thought about how *he* was going to feel when she was gone.

"You've even named him, haven't you?" her mom said. "You called him

Baxter just now. Julie said she tries not to name the puppies."

"I didn't mean to...," Daisy said quietly.

"I think you need to stop spending so much time with him," her mom told her gently. "He'll be going to his new owners soon. He needs to love them, Daisy. Not you."

Daisy nodded slowly. Mom was right. She'd have to play with all the puppies, not just Baxter, so that he didn't think he was her special one.... Daisy sniffed. She couldn't do it. She knew she couldn't. He *was* special!

She'd just have to stop seeing the puppies altogether.

She stood up, and Baxter followed her, his ears twitching anxiously.

Something was wrong. Daisy's voice had changed, and her eyes looked all shiny. He whimpered, and Daisy patted him, but not the way she usually did. It was almost as though she didn't want to touch him anymore. Baxter laid his ears back and looked up at her worriedly. But Daisy wasn't looking at him.

"I'll take him back," she whispered. "Sorry, Baxter...."

Chapter Four

Baxter sat by the wire front of the pen, watching the door out to the yard. The top half of the stable door was open, and two of his brothers were dozing in a patch of warm sun, while the others played. But Baxter didn't want to leave his watch to join in. It was hard to tell when someone was going to open the door, because there were footsteps going past all the time, people wandering across the yard to the shop and the craft workshops. But he was listening anyway, waiting for Daisy to come back.

She hadn't been to see him for a long time, and he didn't understand why. Until a couple of days ago, she'd come to the puppy pen every day to cuddle him, or play games with all the puppies. But especially with him. She really loved him; he could tell from the way she looked at him.

It had all changed after they'd gone out for their walk in the yard. He didn't know what had happened, but everything had gone wrong.

Baxter slumped down by the fence, resting his head on his paws and watching the other puppies tumbling around, chasing after a rope toy. Suddenly, his ears twitched. There was a scuffling noise at the door. Was someone coming? Maybe it was Daisy!

The door opened, and Baxter sprang up, jumping at the wire and scratching at it with his paws.

It wasn't Daisy after all — just Julie, with a man and a boy he hadn't seen before. "Oh, that one's excited!" the man said. As soon as he saw them, Baxter dropped down, and stood gazing sadly out through the wire.

"He's a very sweet puppy, very friendly," Julie said, smiling. But as she opened the pen, Baxter slunk away into the corner, leaving his brothers and sisters to get the attention from the visitors.

"I think I saw his picture on the website!" The little boy pointed to Baxter. "He's the one with the floppy ear. Please, can we have him?"

"Is he all right?" the dad asked, as his son crouched down to look at Baxter. "He doesn't look very friendly. Don't get too close, Davey."

Julie was frowning. "He's usually very affectionate," she said.

"Can I pet him?" asked Davey.

Julie smiled. "Of course you can."

But when Davey tried to pet Baxter, the puppy wriggled further into the corner of the pen.

"I don't think he likes me," Davey said sadly. Just then, one of Baxter's sisters rubbed her head against his knees, making him laugh. "But this puppy's nice, Dad!" He sat down on the floor to pay attention to her, and she climbed into his lap, licking his hands excitedly.

His dad laughed. "I think she's chosen you, Davey." He glanced over at Baxter. "I hope the other puppy's okay."

Julie smiled. "I'm sure he's just having an off-day," she said. But she couldn't help feeling surprised. This little one was usually so friendly — maybe he was missing Daisy? Daisy's mom had explained that she thought Daisy was getting too attached to the puppies and it would be better if she didn't spend so much time with them. Julie had agreed — but she hadn't realized that this puppy had already bonded with Daisy, too.

Daisy's mom did all she could to cheer Daisy up, but she wasn't having much success. Everything seemed to remind Daisy of Baxter. She wouldn't go back to see the puppies at all. She said it made her too sad. Her mom almost wished she hadn't said anything, but then the end of the vacation would have been heartbreaking if she'd let Daisy go on falling in love with Baxter.

"I've booked a surprise for you today," Mom told her, as she passed her the box of cornflakes on Wednesday morning. They were just about used to eating in folding camp chairs by now — it was a weird juggling act, trying to pour cereal and milk, and not tip the bowl into your lap. Dad said that if they came camping again, they'd need a folding table, too.

Daisy was pretty sure she *didn't* want to come again. Even to a different campsite. It would remind her too much of Baxter. Still, she was trying not to be upset and ruin the vacation for Mom and Dad and Oliver. "What is it?" she asked, making herself sound interested.

"Horseback riding!" Mom said. "I saw a brochure at the reception area."

"I don't want to go horseback riding, Mom." Oliver looked up from his cereal. "I said I'd go and play soccer with Liam and Tom."

Mom frowned. "Which ones are Liam and Tom?"

"Mo-om!" Oliver sighed. "They're in the red tent at the other end of our row."

"Well, that's good because I didn't book the horseback riding for you anyway." Mom grinned at him. "I didn't think it was your sort of thing. Daisy and I are going together."

Daisy smiled at her. She knew how hard Mom was trying to make her happy. She did love horses, and she'd wanted to try riding for a long time.

"Actually, we should finish up breakfast quickly," Mom said, checking her watch. "We have a reservation for 10."

The stables were about a 10-minute drive from the campsite. Somehow, Daisy felt a little better once they'd driven out of the Riverside gate. She was still really missing Baxter — especially as she kept wondering if he was missing her, too. But she could squash the sadness down inside her, and be just a little bit excited about going to the stables.

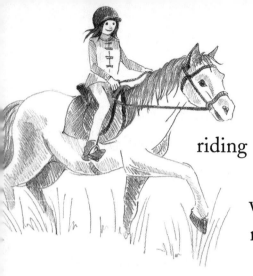

The horseback riding was wonderful. Daisy's pony was a gray one named Shadow, who was very well-behaved. He also seemed to know the paths they were taking, so Daisy didn't feel as if she had to worry about where they were going. Mom's chestnut pony, Cracker, was a little more of a handful. She kept trying to stop and eat mouthfuls of grass, which made Mom slide forward. At one point Mom had had to hang on to Cracker's neck to keep herself from falling into a prickly-looking hedge!

Carly, the riding instructor, kept telling Mom to pull Cracker's reins so that she would leave the grass alone. By the time they got back to the stables, Mom told Daisy that she thought she might have pulled her arms out of their sockets!

They helped to rub the ponies down, and they were just saying good-bye when Daisy gasped.

"What's the matter?" Mom asked.

Daisy didn't say anything. She was staring at a beautiful German shepherd, who was standing at the door to one of the stalls. A dark bay horse was leaning out, and it looked as if they were talking to each other.

"That's Frankie," Carly said. "He's our stable dog. Isn't he beautiful? He goes on the rides sometimes, too. He really loves Pepper, the bay horse over there.

63

If Pepper's out, he follows along." She smiled at Daisy and her mom. "Actually, you're staying at Riverside, aren't you? That's where he came from."

Daisy tried to smile. "Really?" she whispered. Frankie was probably related to Baxter somehow. "Can we go now?" she muttered to Mom.

Mom hugged her. "Of course we can. Oh, Daisy. I'm really sorry...."

All the fun of the horseback riding was swallowed up by how much Daisy was missing Baxter. She was never going to see what he looked like when he was all grown up, like Frankie. She brushed her arm across her eyes to rub away her tears. Why was she being so silly? She'd known all along they'd never be able to take Baxter home. Mom and Dad hadn't even said for sure that they could get a dog, just that they were going to talk about it. And Baxter almost belonged to someone else anyway. But seeing Frankie had made it all seem so much worse.

At least they only had two more days at the campsite. *This was the worst vacation ever*, Daisy thought miserably as she trudged back to the car. And only a couple days ago, she'd thought it couldn't get any better.

Chapter Five

By the next day, Baxter was sick of waiting by the front of the pen. Why had Daisy stopped coming to see him? What if there was something wrong? He prowled around the run all day, sniffing the edges of the pen and trying to find a way out. He needed to go and find Daisy. He was sure she was still somewhere close.

Baxter hardly ate any of the meals that Julie gave him. As usual, she brought the puppies their last meal of the day from the farmhouse at about nine. As she put the bowls down in the pen, Baxter didn't race over like the others. He just went on sniffing carefully at the wire.

Julie shook her head and looked at him worriedly. "I really hope you cheer up a bit before tomorrow," she said, kneeling down next to the puppy to pet him. "Your new owner's coming to see you. She called me today to tell me she's chosen you from those photos I emailed her. She's been waiting for the perfect puppy for a while, she said, and she thinks you're the one. She wants to take you to dog shows."

Baxter nuzzled her hand gently. He might be miserable, but he still liked Julie. He thumped his tail on the scruffy grass of the pen.

"Good boy," Julie said. "Are you missing Daisy? Her mom said she was getting too fond of you, and she was worried it was going to make it hard for her to say good-bye." She sighed. "I probably shouldn't have let her come to see you so much, but she was having such a nice time.... Oh dear, I think that's what it is, isn't it?" She rubbed his ears. "Don't worry. You'll have a wonderful new owner soon."

As she stood up, Baxter sighed and lay down by the wire of the pen, looking out at the yard. Julie frowned. He really *was* missing Daisy. And she was sure Daisy would really be missing him, too.

Julie walked out of the gate, latching it carefully behind her. As she headed back to the farmhouse, she wondered if there was anything she could do to help the puppy.

She didn't notice Baxter's ears twitching curiously. One of them pricked right up, and the other followed suit but then flopped over again the way it always did.

He'd found a hole in the wire fence.

Daisy lay on her tummy at the edge of the river, watching the ducks. Oliver had gone off to play soccer again, and Mom and Dad had gone to wash the dishes after dinner. Daisy thought Mom was probably still feeling sorry for her, after she'd been so upset at the stables. She'd suggested that Daisy read a book in the tent, or find some friends to talk to. But Daisy had spent so much time playing with the puppies that she hadn't really made friends around the campsite like Oliver had.

It was starting to get dark, and the ducks swam slowly away. Dinner had been late — the gas stove had taken a long time to boil the water for the pasta — so it would be time to go to bed soon.

She wriggled up onto her elbows and flicked a little stick into the water, watching it float away downstream. Maybe she could find another stick and race herself.... But then she decided that was just boring. And a bit sad.

I'll go and read in a minute, she thought, dipping her fingers in the water and wishing the ducks would come back.

Baxter scratched at the little dip in the packed earth under the wire fence. The run backed onto the path up to the camping area. If he could just get underneath, he was sure he could find Daisy.

The other puppies were still eating, and his mom was over at the farmhouse, so no one noticed him scraping and digging. Finally, he wriggled underneath the wire and out onto the path.

He trotted away, sniffing the long grass and wondering which way to go. He could hear people talking — their voices carrying through the quiet evening, as children were called back into the tents, and their parents settled down to chat for a while before going to bed.

He sniffed again carefully. He couldn't smell Daisy yet, but maybe she would be where he could hear all those voices. He hurried down the path, his tail wagging a little, head down, searching. He could smell the river, although he wasn't sure what it was. It smelled different and exciting, full of the scents of mice and water rats. Then he spotted some ducks, swimming slowly along the far bank, and went faster, eager to get a closer look.

As he was hurrying over the little bridge, he caught Daisy's scent. He stopped dead in his tracks, sniffing the air and looking around hopefully.

She was there! Lying by the water, as though she were waiting for him! He was so desperate to see Daisy that going the entire way to the end of the bridge seemed too slow. With a joyful bark, Baxter jumped through the railings, landing just on the bank, his back paws scratching in the damp mud at the water's edge. Kicking up the mud, he raced along the grassy riverbank and threw himself at Daisy, who stared at him in amazement.

"Baxter! It's you!" Daisy hugged him, laughing. She'd heard the bark, and the loud scuffling and splashing, but she'd never thought it would be Baxter coming to find her. "How did you get here? I wonder if Julie's looking for you — did you sneak out somehow?"

Baxter laid his head on her lap and sighed contentedly. She wasn't angry. Whatever had happened to make her stop coming, she still loved him. He could tell from her voice.

"Oh, Baxter, I've really missed you." Daisy ran her hand gently through the thick fur on his back. "I think you've gotten bigger, and it's only been three days since I last saw you."

Baxter wasn't sure what she was saying, but he liked listening to her.

He wriggled himself closer, so that his paws and shoulders were on her lap, too. He wasn't going to let her disappear again.

Daisy frowned. "I'm not supposed to be around you. Mom says." She swallowed, feeling a lump rising in her throat. "And she's probably right. She thought it was just going to make both of us miserable. I'm going home soon, you see...."

She knew she should take Baxter back to the farmhouse and tell Julie he'd gotten out somehow. But she couldn't. Not just yet. She wanted to cuddle him a little bit longer. Only until Mom and Dad came back from doing the dishes....

But then they might say it was time

for bed, and Dad would take Baxter back instead. Daisy shook her head suddenly. She knew she couldn't let that happen. Mom was right — she was just making it harder for herself, but she didn't care. Being away from Baxter hadn't stopped her from missing him. It didn't look like he'd forgotten about her, either; he'd obviously come to find her. Would another day of being around him really make it any worse for them both?

Daisy gathered Baxter into her arms and stood up. "You're so heavy," she whispered to him lovingly, and Baxter licked her ear. He liked being carried. "Come on. Mom and Dad will be back soon. And Oliver. We're going to have to be a little sneaky."

For just one night she could pretend that Baxter was *her* dog.... Daisy carried him around to the back of their tent, to her own secret door, and put him down beside her while she unzipped it. Then she crawled inside, calling to Baxter to follow her.

He pattered in happily, sniffing around the funny little room, before slumping down on her sleeping bag.

"Good idea," Daisy muttered. "I'll tell Mom and Dad I'm tired. Are you hungry, Baxter?" she whispered, remembering the nearly full pack of dog treats that was still in her pocket.

She hadn't been able to throw it away. "Julie said she usually gives you supper at about nine. Did she leave the gate open afterward?" Daisy frowned. She couldn't imagine Julie doing that. She was so careful. "I know I should take you back, but I can't. Not yet. I'll take you first thing tomorrow."

She fed Baxter a handful of treats, and watched him gulping them down while she put on her pajamas, and slipped into her sleeping bag.

Baxter sniffed thoughtfully around the walls of the tent, and then lay down next to Daisy, staring up at her, his dark eyes glinting in the dim evening light.

Daisy rubbed his head and Baxter wriggled, his ears twitching. Then Daisy heard what he'd heard — voices.

79

Mom and Dad were on their way back. They mustn't see him!

Quickly, she arranged her fleece blanket half over her sleeping bag and half over Baxter, so he looked like some of her stuff. In this light, when Mom looked in to check on Daisy, she'd never be able to tell there was a dog in there.

"Shhh…," she whispered, feeding him another treat. "You're my secret, okay?"

Baxter scarfed down the treat, and then snuggled closer to her. He didn't mind being quiet, as long as he was with Daisy.

Chapter Six

Daisy woke up early, blinking in the soft sunlight that was coming through the side of the tent. She felt deliciously warm and very happy, but she couldn't quite figure out why.

Then Baxter wriggled and yawned next to her, and she remembered.

"Are you awake, Daisy?" her mom called. "You went to sleep really early last night. Are you feeling okay?"

"I'm fine," Daisy called back, tossing the blanket over Baxter, in case her mom decided to look in and check on her. "Can I go for a walk before breakfast, Mom?"

"I suppose so...." Mom sounded surprised.

"We're going home tomorrow," Daisy added. "I just want to make sure I — um — see everything...."

"You're crazy," Oliver muttered from deep inside his sleeping bag. He hated getting up in the morning.

"I'll be back soon," Daisy promised, flinging on some clothes and unzipping her secret door. Baxter stuck his nose out as soon as she'd opened the zipper enough, sniffing happily at the damp grass.

"Come on," Daisy whispered. "Julie gets up early to feed you. She'll probably have noticed you're missing by now."

She hurried over the bridge, with Baxter pattering after her, his little shiny black claws clicking on the wood.

"Ugh, it's cold." Daisy shivered, wishing she'd looked at the weather before she'd put on her denim shorts. At least she'd brought a hoodie. "I think it might rain," she added sadly. "On our last day." She swallowed. Her last day at Riverside. After tomorrow, she wouldn't be able to see Baxter again.

For a moment, she was tempted to run back to the tent and try to hide him, somehow smuggle him into the car and take him home. But she knew it would never work. It was just a silly daydream.

"Baxter!" she called, hurrying down the path. She wanted to get this over with.

Baxter trotted behind her, his head hanging a little. He could tell where they were going. He didn't want to return to the pen with his brothers and sisters. He'd liked being with Daisy much more.

Daisy had decided she'd better take Baxter to the front door of the farmhouse, as the door in the yard would still be locked. She wasn't quite sure what she was going to say — just that she'd found the puppy. Which was true, even if it wasn't the whole truth. She slowed down as she came up the path, suddenly worrying that Julie might ask her difficult questions.

Baxter hung back at the gate and whined, wishing he were still in the tent. He wanted to snuggle up next to Daisy and have some more of those treats. There was a strong wind blowing, and he didn't like the feel of it whistling around his ears at all.

Daisy came over and picked him up gently. "I know," she muttered in his ear.

"I don't want to leave you, either. But you're not mine, Baxter." She sniffed and knocked on the front door.

It flew open almost at once, and Julie was there with a phone in her hand.

"Oh! He's here. It's all right! Yes, Daisy's got him! I'll call you back in a minute." She ended the call, and hugged Daisy and Baxter. "That was Amy. She'd gone to look along the road for me; we were worried he might have gotten out there. Oh, Daisy, where did you find him?"

"Um, he found me," Daisy told her. "By the river."

"Thank you so much. I went in to feed the puppies this morning, and realized he was gone. He'd dug a little hole under the wire of the run; I don't know how he squeezed himself out." She patted Baxter gently. "I really thought we might have lost you. I'm going to have to block up that hole, aren't I?" She looked Baxter over anxiously. "He's all right? He wasn't limping or anything, was he?"

Daisy shook her head. "He looks fine to me."

"His new owner is coming to see him today, which just made it all worse — can you imagine having to explain that we'd lost him!" Julie sighed. "At least, I hope she'll be his new owner. I've not actually met her yet, but she sounds very nice."

Daisy nodded, and tried to blink away the tears that had suddenly filled her eyes. "Is she going to take him today?" she managed to ask.

Julie put an arm around her. "No. She just wants to meet him. I'm sure she'll be nice, Daisy. He'll have a wonderful home. And you'll get a dog of your own soon. I told your mom and dad how helpful you were, and how you'd be a terrific dog owner."

"Thanks," Daisy said quietly. But it wasn't the same. She wanted Baxter, and she knew she couldn't have him. Blinking away her tears, she passed the furry bundle to Julie, and Baxter whimpered, wriggling back toward her.

"I'd better go. I just went for a walk before breakfast. Mom doesn't know where I am."

"Come and see us later," Julie suggested. "I want to give you something to say thank you."

Daisy nodded and hurried off up the path.

Baxter stared after her, whining miserably. He'd gone and found Daisy, and she'd been happy to see him. Why was she leaving him again?

"That's really nice of Julie," Mom said, when Daisy explained about going over to the farmhouse later. "You just found Baxter wandering along by the river?"

"Yes." Daisy nodded. She had. She just hadn't been very clear about *when*, that was all. "And so I took him back."

Mom eyed her thoughtfully, and Daisy tried not to turn red as she ate her cereal. She was pretty sure that Mom thought there was more going on than she was telling.

"I'm supposed to be going canoeing on the river this morning," Oliver said dismally, staring out from under the canopy at the dark gray sky. As Daisy walked back from the farmhouse, it had started to rain.

Dad shrugged. "Well, you're going to get wet anyway...."

Oliver made a face. "I know. It just doesn't feel like vacation weather anymore, that's all."

"Maybe it'll blow over," Mom said. But it didn't look like it would.

Daisy walked down to the canoe shed with Oliver and Dad later that morning, while Mom went to the village shops. Daisy was going to go over to the farmhouse once she'd watched Oliver for a little while. It was nice of Julie to want to give her something, but it was making her feel a bit guilty.

It took a while for the canoeing to get started. Oliver had to be given a life jacket and paddle, and told all the safety rules. The instructor kept suggesting that Daisy join in, too. In the end, she told Dad she was going to the farmhouse, just to get away before she was forced into a canoe.

When she went back up to the farmhouse, Julie was already talking to someone — and Daisy gulped, remembering what Julie had said.

It was Baxter's new owner.

Daisy didn't really like the look of her. *That might be because I'm jealous*, Daisy thought, trying to be fair. But it seemed strange that the woman was in a fancy dress, when she was coming to see a litter of muddy-pawed puppies. Her frilly umbrella kept trying to turn inside out, too. Daisy hung around by the gate, trying not to get in the way, but now it seemed as though the woman was leaving.

Julie folded her arms and watched as the woman went down the path. She looked a little annoyed. Daisy wondered whether Julie had discovered that Baxter had stayed in her tent all night. But Julie smiled when she saw her.

"Was that Bax — I mean, the puppy's new owner?" Daisy asked her in a small voice.

Julie shook her head. "No. It should have been. But she's decided she doesn't want him after all."

"Why not?" Daisy stared at her. How could anybody not want him?

"Because of his floppy ear. She's looking for a show dog, you see. It would disqualify him in the show ring."

"But you said he'd grow out of it." Daisy frowned.

"Yes, he probably will. But he's the only one of the litter whose ears haven't straightened up, and she thinks it won't. So — she doesn't want him."

Daisy's eyes widened, as thoughts swirled around her head. "But … does that mean he's still for sale?" she stammered, looking up at Julie in sudden hope.

"Well, yes — there's no one else on the waiting list at the moment, so he is, I suppose. Oh! Daisy, come back, I've got some candy for you!"

But Daisy was gone, racing back along the path to the river, to tell her dad that they had to give Baxter a home.

Chapter Seven

"Dad! Dad! You have to come!" Daisy dashed up to where her dad was huddled in his raincoat, watching Oliver, who was out on the river now.

"What's the matter?" Dad looked worried, but Daisy laughed.

"Nothing! Nothing's the matter. It's a good thing! Baxter's new owner doesn't want him. We can buy him!

We could take him home with us tomorrow! You have to come and talk to Julie."

"What? Slow down, Daisy, I don't understand." Dad was frowning, and for the first time since Julie had told her the news, Daisy stopped to think. She'd been so excited that Baxter was for sale again that she hadn't even considered whether her parents would say yes.

"Baxter … the German shepherd puppy — the one I really like. I had to stop seeing him because he was going to belong to someone else, and it wasn't fair to him. But he isn't anyone's now, Dad!"

"What are you two talking about that's so important?"

Daisy jumped. Mom had come up behind her without her even noticing.

"Daisy says that the puppy…," Dad began. He sounded worried.

"It's Baxter, Mom." Daisy's words were tumbling over each other as she tried to explain. "The lady who was supposed to buy him changed her mind. So we can have him — can't we? You said you were seriously thinking about getting a dog. Please, please can it be *this* dog?"

"But Daisy, a great big German shepherd?" Her mom sighed. "I know he's cute and little and fluffy now, but think how big Lucy and Sally are! We couldn't have a dog like that."

"Why not?" Daisy swallowed hard. She couldn't cry now. She needed to persuade them, and they'd never listen if she were crying.

"Well, our yard isn't big enough. The house isn't big enough, either, come to think of it! Imagine a huge dog in our living room, Daisy. He'd take up the entire sofa."

"He wouldn't be allowed on the sofa, Mom. We'd train him properly, like Julie said. So he wouldn't make a mess and stuff. He wouldn't be like Melissa's dog." Daisy dug her nails into the palms of her hands, forcing herself to sound calm and sensible. "There's a dog-training class that meets in the same hall as Brownies. I've seen a poster. And we're so close to the park. I'm almost old enough to take him there on my own."

Her mom shook her head. "I'm not sure about that."

"Well, okay, with Oliver then. And I *will* be old enough soon." She turned to her dad. "You said you wanted to go for walks with a dog, Dad!"

Dad sighed. "I do, Daisy. This is all just a bit sudden. And your mom's right. We never thought of having such a big dog. German shepherds need lots of exercise, and they're bred to be working dogs. I'm not sure they're great pets."

"But you don't know Baxter," Daisy pleaded. "Not like I do. He'd be a wonderful pet." She was losing, she could tell. Mom and Dad didn't understand; they weren't listening. Tears started to stream down her face.

"Don't cry, Daisy." Mom went to put an arm around her, but Daisy pulled away and ran off back to the tent.

How could this be happening?

Baxter could be hers, after all, but she was going to lose him.

Baxter prowled up and down the run, the fur on the back of his neck prickling. He hated being back in his pen, even though he'd been happy to see the other puppies again. He wanted to be back up at the campsite with Daisy.

Especially now. It was still raining heavily, and the wind was picking up, too. He didn't like the feel of it. It was really howling through the pen, and whistling around the yard, too, rattling all the doors and making the puppies jump and whimper.

He needed to go back to Daisy, and make sure she was all right. But Julie had carefully blocked up the hole under the wire fence, digging a board in so he couldn't get out that way again.

He was stuck.

"You'll just have to share Otto with me instead," Oliver said, grinning. "I'll let you feed him, if you like. Spiders don't need walking all the time."

He was smirking at her over his bowl of soup, and suddenly Daisy couldn't stand it any longer. They'd been stuck in the tent in the pouring rain for a while, and Oliver was driving her crazy. She'd tried being calm and persuasive and sensible, and everyone had treated her like a silly little girl who didn't know what she was talking about.

Okay, fine. So she would be a silly little girl. It didn't matter, anyway. Mom and Dad had refused to listen to any more discussion about Baxter. Mom had said that no meant no, as though Daisy were about three. Mom had even gone to see Julie, and explained that as much as they'd love a dog, they just couldn't have one as big and demanding as a German shepherd.

"I hate you and your dumb spider!" Daisy screamed. She flung herself at Oliver, not even noticing that she'd spilled the tomato soup all down his front. His folding chair tipped over and they both fell to the ground.

"Daisy, stop it!" Mom yelled, and Dad pulled her off Oliver, looking furious.

"Look at you both!" he snapped. "You'd better go to bed, Daisy. And you, too!" he added, as Oliver snickered. "You were teasing her. I'm going to be really glad to get out of this tent and get home tomorrow."

Daisy zipped herself into her pod, changed out of her dirty hoodie and shorts, and crawled into her sleeping bag. She buried her face in the fleece blanket she'd used to cover up Baxter. It still smelled like him. She couldn't stop crying now. She hated it that Oliver and Mom and Dad could hear her. Maybe the drumming of the rain on the tent and the howling of the wind would hide the crying a little.

Baxter was so close. That was the awful thing. Just across the river and down the path. He would be curling up to go to sleep with the other puppies now. She could almost see him....

But they were going home tomorrow, and then she'd never see him again.

Baxter shook his ears worriedly. Julie had closed the door out to the run when she'd come to bring the puppies' dinner because it was raining so hard. But he could still hear it hammering on the roof, and the wind battering around the yard. All the puppies hated the eerie noises.

But he was the only one left awake now. The others had settled into an uneasy sleep, huddled together for comfort. Baxter sat down by the wire fence of the pen and whined miserably. Something was wrong, he was sure of it. All this wind and rain. More than ever, Baxter wanted to be with Daisy. He was scared and she would make him feel better, but that wasn't the real reason he wanted to be with her. He was scared for *her*. The wind had been blowing around the tent even that morning, and he hadn't liked the way it shook. He needed to be there to guard her and keep her safe.

He jumped in fright as a particularly strong gust of wind whistled around the yard and blew the door of the puppy room off its latch. The bottom of the door creaked open, clattering against the wall. It was usually locked at night, but the horrible weather had meant that Julie was racing around, distracted, and she'd forgotten to lock it when she brought the puppies' food from the farmhouse.

The other puppies wriggled and whimpered in their sleep, but none of them woke up. Baxter shivered as the cold wind cut through the room, but then his ears pricked up — or one of them did, anyway.

The door was open now! He could go and find Daisy!

If he could get out of the wire pen….

He scratched at it uselessly, but he only hurt his paws. And it was no good trying to dig under it, as he'd done outside. This was a solid floor. He would have to go over the top of the wire.

Baxter stood on his hind paws, reaching up as far as he could. To his surprise, he was actually as tall as the fence now. His front paws hung over the top, and he could just get his head over it. He kicked and scratched at the floor, trying to push himself up, but he wasn't quite tall enough. Then his claws caught on the bar across the top, and he kicked harder — he was climbing! He scratched again, getting the other back paw up, and heaved himself over the edge of the pen, teetering on the top for a few seconds. Then, almost without realizing how he'd done it, Baxter was on the floor — on the other side of the wire.

He looked nervously at the door. It was still banging back and forth, and it was dark and wet outside. For a moment he wished that he were back inside with his brothers and sisters, where it was warm and safe.

Then he shook himself. He needed to find Daisy. He marched across the floor, and nudged the swinging door hard with his nose.

Out in the yard the rain was

hammering down so hard that he could barely see. Baxter shrank back against the wall, trying to think of how to get to Daisy. When he'd found her before, he'd gone out of the side of the run instead, straight onto the path.

Ears laid back against the driving rain, Baxter set out across the yard to where he thought he remembered the entrance was, his tail tucked between his legs. He'd never seen anything like this before. It had been a hot summer — so hot that all of the ground was dry, and as he reached the path there were huge puddles where the water couldn't soak in fast enough. Baxter hurried around them, shivering as the rain soaked through his thick fur. He was fairly sure he knew where he was going now, but as he came closer to the river his ears laid back even further than before.

It hadn't looked like this yesterday.

The hot weather had left the river low and sluggish, but now the torrential rain had filled it up again, so that it was racing along, sticks and debris jostling around in the dark water. It was starting to overflow its banks, too.

Baxter hesitated at the end of the bridge. Water was lapping around his paws, but he knew that to get to Daisy, he had to go across. The river just seemed so much bigger and scarier now than it had before. It stretched out beyond the bridge on the other side, too, and that was what made Baxter move at last.

On the other side of the bridge was Daisy's tent — and the water had almost reached it.

Chapter Eight

Baxter raced across the bridge, splashing through the water at the end, which was halfway up his legs. The ground sloped up from the river to the tents, but only a little. The moonlight shone on the dark water that was rising slowly but surely toward Daisy's pod.

He reached the tent and barked as loudly as he could, right outside Daisy's secret door. He hated this water — it was black and scary, and he didn't want it anywhere near Daisy.

Inside the tent, Daisy whimpered and turned over in her sleep as she heard Baxter. The barking just merged into her dreams, making them even more terribly real. Baxter was racing along behind the car as they drove away, barking and barking. He didn't understand why she wasn't taking him with her.

Neither did Daisy.

He was out of sight now. Although Daisy was still staring out of the car window, she couldn't see him at all. So why could she still hear him barking?

Daisy sat up suddenly, clutching her sleeping bag around her. That wasn't part of her dream! That was actually Baxter! He'd come to find her again. Smiling, she unzipped her back door.

"Baxter, shhh! You'll wake up Mom and Dad — oh, wow!" Daisy gasped as she saw the floodwater rising up toward the tent.

Baxter whined impatiently. Why was she still sitting there? She needed to get out, and the others, too! He darted into her tent pod and grabbed her sleeve in his teeth, pulling her.

"Baxter, you came to rescue us!" Daisy whispered, staring at him in amazement. "How did you know? Okay, okay." She reached out to unzip her front door, the one that led into the living area. "Mom! Dad! Oliver! The river's flooding! We have to get out of the tent!"

"What?" There was a scuffling noise, then the zipper opened and Dad's head appeared around the door.

"It really is! Baxter came to tell us, Dad. He's outside. He barked to wake me up!"

Dad dashed across the living area into Daisy's pod, and stared out silently for a moment. Then he turned around and dashed back, grabbing his boots. "I don't how that dog knew, or how he got here, but it's lucky he did. Your mom's just getting dressed. The water will be in the tent any minute. Oliver, up, now! We need to get out of the tent!"

"Where are we going?" Daisy asked, padding across the living area to grab her boots and raincoat.

Dad frowned. "The farmhouse. We need to let them know the river's flooding. I'm sure they'll find somewhere for us to sleep. And help us get our stuff out, too. But I'm going to go and tell the people in the tents closest first." He hurried out, pulling on his raincoat over his pajamas as he unzipped the front of the tent.

Baxter was standing in the doorway of Daisy's pod, watching anxiously. He wanted her out of there now, before that black water came any closer.

"He really came to tell you what was happening?" Oliver said as he struggled out of his pod, still sounding sleepy.

Daisy nodded proudly. "He must have gotten out of the puppy room again."

"That's amazing." Oliver patted Baxter, but he hardly noticed. The water was getting closer and closer. He barked warningly at Daisy, and pulled at the leg of her pajamas with his teeth.

"He wants you to get out of here," Mom said, appearing from her pod. "Get your boots on, Oliver. We'd better go."

Daisy patted her leg and stepped outside. "Come on, Baxter."

It was eerie watching the water creeping up the grass toward the tents. Dad had woken up the families in all the tents closest to the water, and they were starting to come out, dressed in boots and raincoats.

Baxter stood in front of Daisy's tent, looking nervously at the water. They needed to get back across the bridge, but he hated the thought of going across the flooded bank. It would be high up his legs by now. He glanced up at Daisy, her face white in the darkness. She looked scared, too. He whined and took a couple of steps toward the bridge. He had to get her to the farmhouse, where she'd be safe.

Dad came hurrying back with his flashlight. "Good dog. We're coming now."

Daisy could hear the other families coming along behind him, the children pointing Baxter out as the dog who'd woken everyone up to rescue them.

"Is he your dog?" one of the boys Oliver played soccer with asked her admiringly.

Daisy caught her breath, staring hopefully up at her dad. He nodded. "After this, I think he is," he muttered. "I don't care how big he's going to get. He's a hero."

"They're trained to be rescue dogs, aren't they?" Mom said. "I can see why. Come on. We'll figure out how we're going to manage when we're back on dry land."

Daisy put her hand on Baxter's back. *Her* puppy's back. Dad was holding her other hand tightly, as though he didn't want to let her go.

Baxter looked up at Daisy, and splashed forward into the water, head down, determined. He was going to make sure Daisy was safe, even if it meant going back across the river.

"It's almost coming over the bridge," Daisy said to Dad.

Dad nodded. "We need to tell them at the farm, fast. Then they can get around in the truck over the other bridge, and make sure everyone's okay." He grinned at Daisy as they followed Baxter off the bridge, through the water again to the path on the other side. "We'd better tell them we've got this little one, as well."

"And that we're keeping him?" Daisy said, hesitantly. Had Mom and Dad really meant it?

But her dad nodded. "And that we're keeping him," he agreed.

Daisy gripped the thick fur under her fingers even tighter. Baxter looked up at her, his ears twitching with relief as they came out of the water at last. Holding his head up high, he set off down the path, leading them all the way to somewhere safe and dry.

"Look!" Daisy pointed further down the path — lights were coming toward them from the farmhouse, and anxious voices were calling. "It must be Julie. They're coming to get us."

Dad hugged her. "We'll have to tell her she's too late, Daisy. We've already been rescued!"

"I still can't believe the river rose that quickly." Julie shook her head. "It's never been that high. We were lucky there were only a few tents close enough to be flooded."

"Did everyone manage to get their

stuff out?" Daisy's mom asked.

Julie nodded. "It's all drying in the stables. And most people are heading home today, like you, so they had to spend only one night in our spare rooms, and the empty cottage. I don't think we'll use that end of the field for camping again, though — it could have been so much worse."

Daisy yawned, leaning against Mom's arm. She'd spent the rest of last night sleeping on Julie's living-room floor, wrapped up in spare blankets. She'd let Oliver have the sofa — she had wanted Baxter next to her, and she didn't want him to get into bad habits. She wasn't going to do anything that might make Mom and Dad angry.

Baxter didn't look tired at all.

His eyes were sparkling, and he kept twisting his head around to look at the collar and leash that Julie had given Daisy for him. She said they'd need them when they stopped to let him out on the way home.

Home! Daisy smiled to herself. She still could hardly believe it. Dad was packing the car now, carefully making a safe space in the back for Baxter. It meant Daisy and Oliver would have a lot of bags around their legs, but they didn't mind.

"I think we're ready," Dad said. "Julie, do you think he has enough room in here?"

Julie looked over. "He should be fine." She smiled at Daisy. "I'm so glad he's going home with you. It's perfect."

Daisy lifted Baxter into the car, patting him gently as she took off his leash. "I can't believe he's really ours," she told Julie, giggling as Baxter licked her cheek. "Not just for the vacation, but forever."